For my mother and father

*I would like to thank Helen Read for the
decorative borders she designed and
painted so beautifully.*

F.M.

The Honey Hunters is an adaptation of a traditional tale
told by the Ngoni people of Africa.

Text copyright © 1992 by Walker Books
Illustrations copyright © 1992 by Francesca Martin

First U.S. edition 1992
First published in Great Britain in 1992
by Walker Books Ltd., London.
ISBN 1-56402-086-X
Library of Congress Catalog Card Number 91-58736
Library of Congress Cataloging in Publication
information is available.

10 9 8 7 6 5 4 3 2 1

Printed in Hong Kong by
South China Printing Co. (1988) Ltd.

The pictures in this book are watercolor paintings.

Candlewick Press
2067 Massachusetts Avenue
Cambridge, Massachusetts 02140

The Honey Hunters

A traditional African tale illustrated by
Francesca Martin

CANDLEWICK PRESS
CAMBRIDGE, MASSACHUSETTS

Once upon a time, all the wild animals
were the greatest of friends. And, as it
happened, they all loved honey. The little
gray honey guide knew the best places to find honey.
"Che, che! Cheka, cheka, che!" the bird would cry.
"If you want honey, follow me!"

One day a boy was walking by the lake
when he heard the honey guide's song.
"I'd like some honey," he said. "I'll follow you."
And so the boy and the honey guide set off
together through the bush.

Soon they met a rooster.

"Che, che! Cheka, cheka, che!" sang the
honey guide. "If you want honey, follow me!"
"I'd like some honey," said the rooster, fluffing
up his tail feathers. "I'll follow you."
And so the rooster joined the boy as he followed
the honey guide through the bush.

They had not gone far

when they saw a bush cat.

"Che, che! Cheka, cheka, che!" sang the

honey guide. "If you want honey, follow me!"

"I'd like some honey," said the bush cat,

dropping from the tree. "I'll follow you."

So the honey guide and the boy and the rooster

and the bush cat set off together.

By and by they
met an antelope . . .   and then
                              a leopard . . .   and then
                                                        a zebra . . .

and then
a lion . . .

"Che, che! Cheka, cheka, che!" the honey guide sang to each of the animals. "If you want honey, follow me!" So the antelope and the leopard, the zebra and the lion, joined the boy and the rooster and the bush cat as they followed the honey guide through the bush.

Soon the animals met an elephant.

"Where are you all going, my friends?" he asked.

"To find some honey," replied the boy.

"Che, che! Cheka, cheka, che!" sang the honey guide.

"If you want honey, follow me!"

So the elephant joined the procession
of animals going in search of honey.

In a short while, the honey guide stopped.

"Che, che! Cheka, cheka, che!" he sang again.

"If you want honey, look in this tree!"

Then the boy took a beautiful honeycomb

from the bees' nest and broke it into four pieces.

The first he gave to the rooster and the bush cat.

The second he gave to the antelope and the leopard.

The third he gave to the zebra and the lion.

And the fourth he kept for himself and the elephant.

Then all the animals began to eat . . .

The rooster pecked his
end of the honeycomb
and the bush cat licked his.
Then the bush cat spat at
the rooster and the rooster
scratched the bush cat.

The antelope nibbled her
end of the honeycomb
and the leopard gulped his.
Then the leopard clawed the
antelope and the antelope
kicked the leopard.

The zebra chewed her end of the honeycomb and the lion tore off a big chunk. Then the lion leapt upon the zebra and the zebra bit the lion with her sharp teeth.

The elephant seized the honeycomb from the boy and swallowed it whole. And the boy just stared in amazement at the squabbling animals.

"Stop!" the boy cried. "Don't fight!

You have never quarreled with each other before!"

But the animals refused to listen.

In desperation the boy picked up a stick

and waved it at them.

At this, the animals fell silent.

The elephant turned to the boy and said sadly,

"The damage is done. We can never be friends again.

From now on, the rooster will fight the bush cat,

the antelope will fight the leopard, the zebra will

fight the lion, and I will fight you and all your kind."

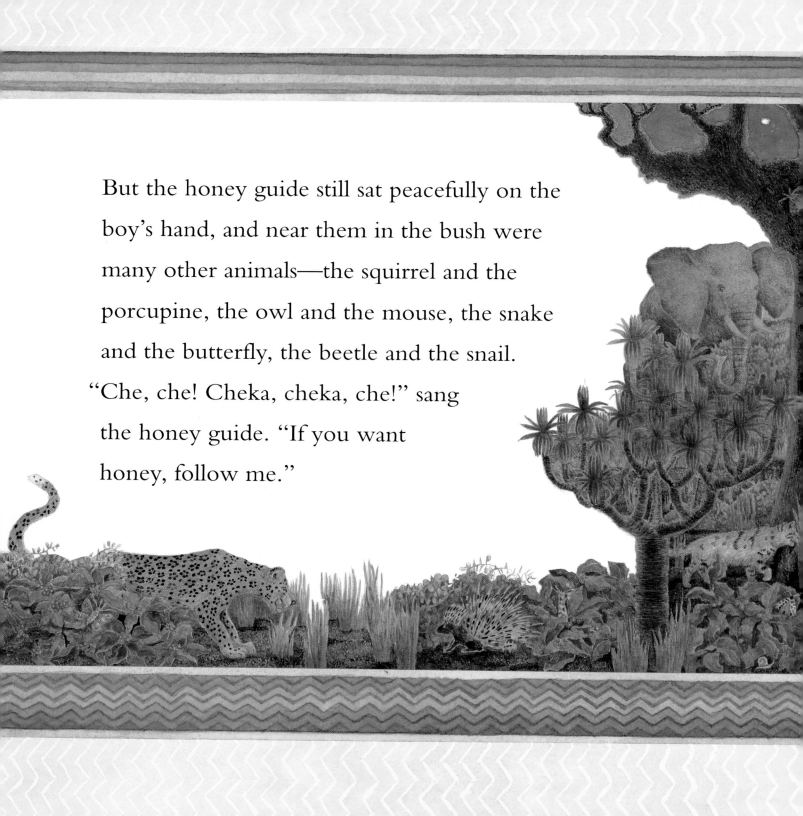

But the honey guide still sat peacefully on the
boy's hand, and near them in the bush were
many other animals—the squirrel and the
porcupine, the owl and the mouse, the snake
and the butterfly, the beetle and the snail.
"Che, che! Cheka, cheka, che!" sang
the honey guide. "If you want
honey, follow me."